For my father, a tireless walker

The illustrations in this book are hand-drawn using graphite pencil
and watercolour paints, and finished using digital methods

Translated by Polly Lawson. First published in French as *Nous Avons Rendez-Vous* by Éditions du Seuil, Paris in 2018
First published in English by Floris Books, Edinburgh in 2020. First published in the USA in 2021. Fourth printing 2022
© 2018 Editions du Seuil. English text © 2020 Floris Books
All rights reserved. No part of this book may be reproduced without the prior permission of Floris Books, Edinburgh
www.florisbooks.co.uk British Library CIP Data available. ISBN 978-178250-639-3. Printed in Poland through Hussar

Floris Books supports sustainable forest management by
printing this book on materials made from wood that
comes from responsible sources and reclaimed material

THE
NIGHT
WALK

MARIE DORLÉANS

Floris
Books

Mama opened our bedroom door,
interrupting the night-time darkness.

"Wake up, you two," she whispered.
"Let's go, so we get there on time."

We got dressed without talking,
our eyes half-closed.

It was the middle of the night.

Outside, crickets chirped
in corners of the garden.
The summer air smelled of
irises and honeysuckle.

We padded softly through the sleeping village.

The pavements were still warm from the heat of the day.

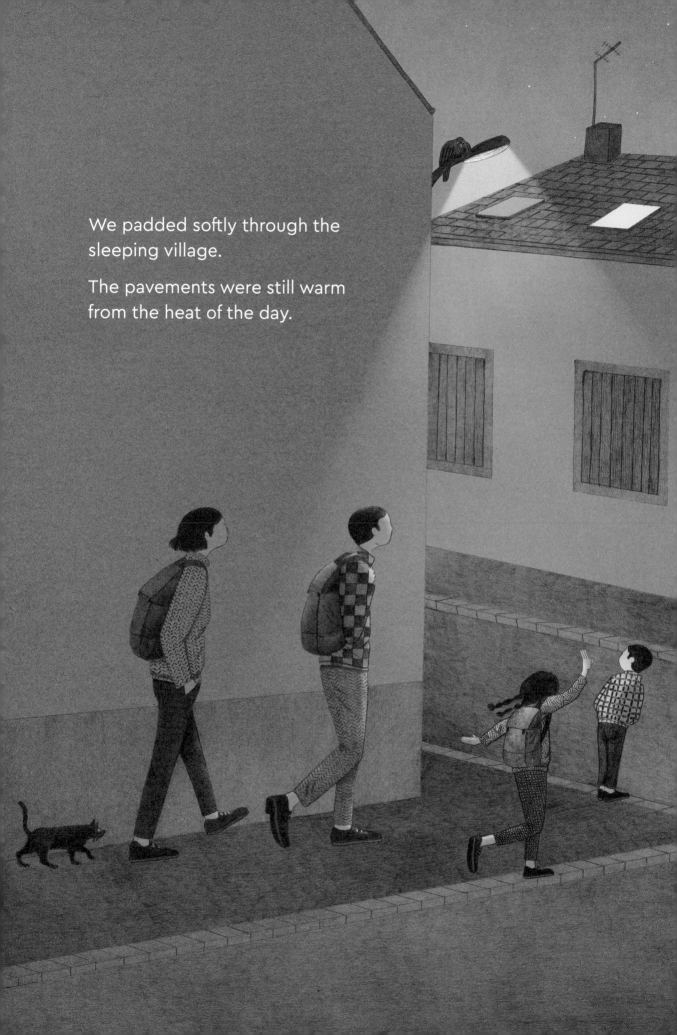

The big hotel was wide awake: it glowed bright like a chandelier...

...but the last house in the village was almost asleep.
It had one eye open.

As we walked deeper into the countryside,
the scent of grass filled our noses.

Little by little, shapes emerged from the
shadows as our eyes adjusted to the night.

We left the road, and the path
climbed gently out of the valley.

A train sliced through the darkness:
wheels shrieking, carriages shaking.

Then it was gone.
There was just us and the still silence.

We threaded through the whispering forest.
The earth was damp, the bark smelled comforting.

Dead branches snapped under our feet,
and ferns swayed quietly as we passed.

We walked slowly, lulled by the rustling of the leaves above.

Then suddenly...

The big hotel was wide awake: it glowed bright like a chandelier...

...but the last house in the village was almost asleep.
It had one eye open.

...a lake!

We stopped to play with the moon.

Further on, we found a clearing.
"Let's lie down," said Mama.

We gasped at the vast, glittering sky.
Grass scratched our backs.

We stayed until Papa said, "Let's push on.
We need to keep walking, so we get
there on time."

We climbed up a hillside, picking
our way from rock to rock.

"Hurry!" said Mama.

We got there just in time.
We watched for a moment.

And then...

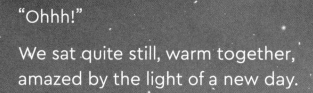

"Ohhh!"

We sat quite still, warm together,
amazed by the light of a new day.

'The Night Walk is a simple and powerful work, that invites us to imagine all the adventures that are possible when the world is sleeping.'

– Nicolas de Crécy, Landerneau Children's Book Prize

Marie Dorléans studied at the School of Decorative Arts in Strasbourg, France. Since her graduation in 2010, she has created children's books as both author and illustrator. *The Night Walk* won the Landerneau Children's Book Prize, was shortlisted for the Prix Sorcières and was a New York Times/New York Public Library Best Illustrated Children's Book in 2021. Marie breathes poetry and delicacy into her stories with realistic, carefully observed illustrations.